# POMPEii

Look for these and other
exciting World Disasters books:

**The Black Death**
**The Titanic**
**The San Francisco Earthquake**
**The Chicago Fire**
**The Dust Bowl**
**The Crash of '29**
**The Armenian Earthquake**

# POMPEii

by
**Timothy Levi Biel**

**Illustrations by**
**Walter Stuart and Chris Miller**

LUCENT
B·O·O·K·S

**WORLD DISASTERS**

PM JL

Library of Congress Cataloging-in-Publication Data

Biel, Timothy L.
    Pompeii.

        (World disasters)
        Bibiliography: p.
        Includes index.
        Summary: Describes the destruction of the city of
Pompeii during the eruption of Mount Vesuvius in A.D. 79.
and how its rediscovery nearly 1700 years later provided in-
formation about life in the Roman Empire.
        1. Pompeii (Ancient city)—Juvenile literature.    2. Italy—
Antiquities—Juvenile literature.    3. Vesuvius (Italy)—
Eruption, 79—Juvenile literature.    [1. Pompeii (Ancient
city)    2. Vesuvius (Italy)—Eruption, 79]
I. Stuart, Walter, 1953-    ill.    II. Miller, Chris,
1957-    ill.    III. Title.    IV. Series.
DG70.P7B55    1989                937'.7                89-9395
ISBN 1-56006-000-X

*To Anga and Justin*

# Table of Contents

## Preface
# The World Disaster Series

World disasters have always aroused human curiosity. Whenever news of tragedy spreads, we want to learn more about it. We wonder how and why the disaster happened, how people reacted, and whether we might have acted differently. To be sure, disaster evokes a wide range of responses — fear, sorrow, despair, generosity, even hope. Yet from every great disaster, one remarkable truth always seems to emerge: in spite of death, pain, and destruction, the human spirit triumphs.

History is full of disasters, arising from a variety of causes. Earthquakes, floods, volcanoes, and other natural events often produce widespread destruction. Just as often, however, people accidentally bring suffering and distress on themselves and other human beings. And many disasters have sinister causes, like human greed, envy, or prejudice.

The disasters included in this series have been chosen not only for their dramatic qualities, but also for their educational value. The reader will learn about the causes and effects of the greatest disasters in history. Technical concepts and interesting anecdotes are explained and illustrated in inset boxes.

But disasters should not be viewed in isolation. To enrich the reader's understanding, these books present historical information about the time period and interesting facts about the culture in which the disaster occurred. Finally, they teach valuable lessons about human nature. More acts of bravery, cowardice, intelligence, and foolishness are compressed into the few days of a disaster than most people experience in a lifetime.

Dramatic illustrations and evocative narrative lure the reader to distant cities and times gone by. Readers witness the awesome power of an exploding volcano, the magnitude of a violent earthquake, and the hopelessness of passengers on a mighty ship passing to its watery grave. By reliving the events, the reader will see how disaster affects the lives of real people and will gain a deeper understanding of their sorrow, their pain, their courage, and their hope.

## Introduction

# The Story of a Lost City

In A.D. 79, the Roman Empire was the mightiest empire on earth. One of the richest, most beautiful, and most visited cities in this great empire was Pompeii.

On the lush, green hillsides of Mt. Vesuvius, overlooking the Mediterranean Sea, stood Pompeii's magnificent mansions and majestic temples. Marble columns two stories high encircled its entire forum, or public square. Wealthy men and women from every corner of the empire gathered here. They came to this city 100 miles (160 kilometers) south of Rome to enjoy a mild climate, splendid scenery, luxurious natural baths, stirring theatrical performances, and other entertainment.

Those who happened to be in Pompeii on the afternoon of August 24, A.D. 79, however, would never leave the city alive. On that day, Mt. Vesuvius was blown apart by a tremendous volcanic eruption. At about 1:00 P.M. the volcano began to spew rocks, ash, and hot poisonous gases on Pompeii. Fires broke out, statues and marble columns collapsed, roofs caved in, and houses,

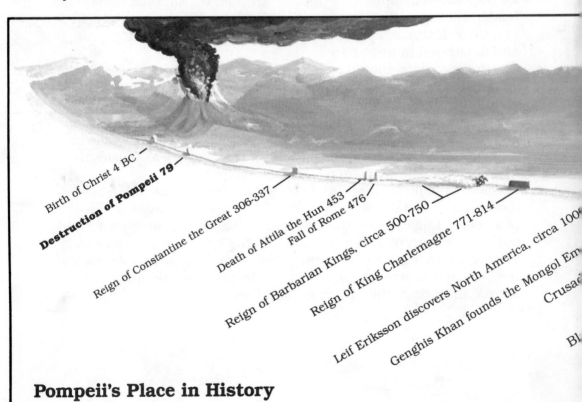

Birth of Christ 4 BC

Destruction of Pompeii 79

Reign of Constantine the Great 306-337

Death of Attila the Hun 453

Fall of Rome 476

Reign of Barbarian Kings, circa 500-750

Reign of King Charlemagne 771-814

Leif Eriksson discovers North America, circa 100

Genghis Khan founds the Mongol Em

Crusa

Bl

**Pompeii's Place in History**

shops, and temples came crashing down. About 10,000 people were killed, and no one saw another trace of Pompeii for nearly 1,700 years.

Then in 1748 began one of the most amazing stories in the history of archaeology. A Spanish engineer named Roque de Alcubierre dug through more than 30 feet (9 meters) of hard volcanic rock on the south face of Mt. Vesuvius. There he discovered a temple from the ancient forum at Pompeii. Word spread quickly that the legendary city had been found. Treasure hunters flocked to the site and began to dig Pompeii out of the rocks and ash that had hidden it for so long. They could not believe what they uncovered.

The rocks and ash that buried Pompeii had also preserved it, just as it looked on the day of the eruption. Many buildings were still standing, their walls still beautifully decorated by ancient Roman paintings and sculptures. Furniture, jewelry, tools, and even food supplies were preserved. Most shocking of all, the hardened ash had preserved life-like forms of many victims killed by the eruption.

Today, archaeologists have made plaster casts of these victims, and they have restored much of Pompeii. They have learned a great deal about ancient Roman life from this historic city. In fact, visiting Pompeii today is like travelling back through time, to the days of the Roman Empire.

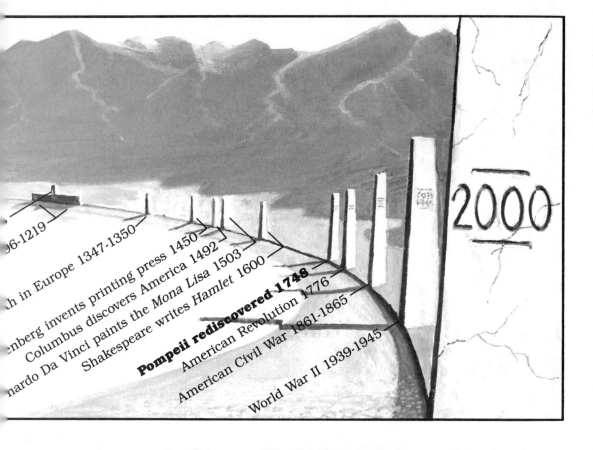

# One
# Entering Pompeii

Imagine arriving in Pompeii by ship in the year A.D. 79. You would be one of many visitors to this beautiful resort city on the slopes of Mt. Vesuvius. It was a favorite vacation spot for Roman emperors and their wealthy subjects.

From its port on the Bay of Naples, you could look up and see the city tucked against the mountain. Elegant mansions with orange tile roofs stood out against the green forest. Majestic temples and marble columns gleamed in the Mediterranean sunlight. Overlooking the bay, on the cliffs of Mt. Vesuvius, were luxurious baths and swimming pools.

As you stepped ashore, you would find yourself in the middle of a busy port. Rough-looking slaves dressed in breeches loaded and unloaded ships. The sweat and grime glistened on their bare chests. Other slaves, dressed in simple gray **tunics**, carried whips and shouted instructions. These were **stewards**, or head slaves.

You would see people from many different ranks of Roman society at the port. Social rank was a big part of Roman life. Everyone in the empire, from the lowest slave to the emperor himself,

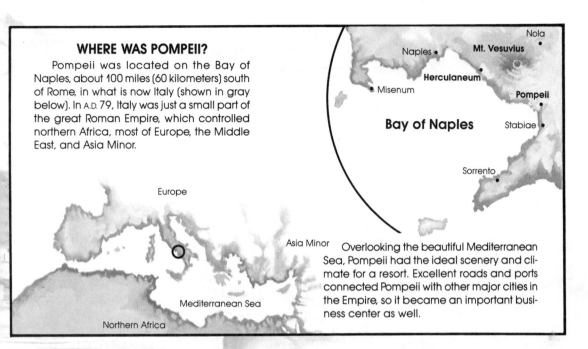

### WHERE WAS POMPEII?

Pompeii was located on the Bay of Naples, about 100 miles (60 kilometers) south of Rome, in what is now Italy (shown in gray below). In A.D. 79, Italy was just a small part of the great Roman Empire, which controlled northern Africa, most of Europe, the Middle East, and Asia Minor.

Nola

Naples •   **Mt. Vesuvius**  •

**Herculaneum**

• Misenum   **Pompeii** •

**Bay of Naples**   Stabiae •

Sorrento •

Europe

Asia Minor   Overlooking the beautiful Mediterranean Sea, Pompeii had the ideal scenery and climate for a resort. Excellent roads and ports connected Pompeii with other major cities in the Empire, so it became an important business center as well.

Mediterranean Sea

Northern Africa

knew his or her place on the social ladder. You could usually tell people's social rank by the clothes they wore and the kind of work they did.

About half the people in Pompeii were slaves. They did most of the hard work, including many jobs that required training and education. They farmed, they built houses, they operated bakeries, fish markets, and other shops. Many teachers, doctors, artists, and actors were slaves. The slaves of wealthy citizens and government officials actually lived better than most free people. Many of them were paid to work, and sometimes they saved enough money to buy their freedom.

Freed slaves were known as *freedmen*. Most merchants, craftsmen, architects, doctors, and teachers were freedmen. These former slaves also conducted much of the business at the port, such as keeping records and exchanging money.

Most freedmen worked for wealthy citizens, but a few went into business for themselves. Those who were successful wore crisp, clean togas and shiny jewelry. A small number of them even reached the highest levels of Roman society.

Members of high society made up a tiny portion of the total population. Despite their small numbers, though, the wealthy citizens were the most influential people in the empire. They were in charge of the government and the imperial armies.

Romans loved to rank people. For instance, there were three distinct orders of wealthy citizens. The highest of these was the Order of **Senators**. Next came the Order of **Decurions**, and finally the Order of **Equestrians**. Ranking depended on a number of qualifications, the most important of which was wealth.

The richest people in the empire belonged to the Order of Senators. Only members of this order could serve in the Roman Senate. In A.D. 79, just 600 of the empire's 60 million inhabitants belonged to this order. They were easy to recognize because they were the only people in the empire allowed to wear togas with a purple border. Among this elite group were several of Pompeii's most prominent citizens.

A step below the Order of Senators was the Order of *Decurions*. The city councilmen in all Roman cities except Rome itself were members of this order. *Decurions* often wore special gold rings

to their families. Their wives, of course, were the best-dressed women in town. They wore full-length, flowing dresses, called **stolas** in many bright colors. They often wore so many rings, earrings, necklaces, bracelets, and hair bands made of gold and precious gems, that they needed several slaves just to dress them and fix their hair.

If you were a wealthy visitor, you might be a guest in one of the **villas**, or country estates, on the outskirts of Pompeii. As you followed the road uphill

## BEGGING IN THE STREETS

Even in Pompeii, wealthy citizens were far outnumbered by thieves and beggars. Most of these were free people who could not find jobs, because slaves did most of the work. In the streets, at the temples, and in front of private homes, poor people begged for meals, clothing, and money.

with an official insignia to identify themselves.

Members of these top two orders often rose through the ranks of the equestrians, who were the highest military officers in the empire. After retiring from a successful military career, an equestrian usually became part of the wealthy governing class.

As a rule, only men belonged to these orders, but the prestige extended from the port to the city, you would first glimpse the bright orange roof of the villa. Then you would see its white stucco walls, two stories high. These walls enclosed an area nearly as large as a football field.

On the outside walls, there were no windows, just a small front porch. In Roman houses, most of the windows and doors opened onto an inner courtyard. This design made the houses difficult to break into, which was important, since there were many thieves in those days. Most home owners kept a slave on duty day and night to guard the main entrance. For added protection, they often had a guard dog chained near the doorway.

A doorman greeted guests at the front entrance and announced their arrival to his master. In the entryway was a small altar dedicated to the **lares**, or household gods. Visitors were expected to offer flowers, incense, or other small gifts at these altars to ward off evil spirits that might have followed them in.

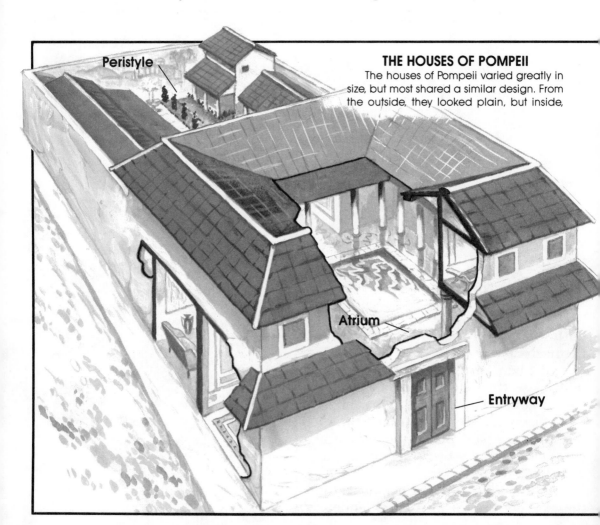

Peristyle

**THE HOUSES OF POMPEII**
The houses of Pompeii varied greatly in size, but most shared a similar design. From the outside, they looked plain, but inside,

Atrium

Entryway

## A ROMAN FARM

A Roman villa, or country home, was nearly as large as a football field. Most of the space within its walls was used for farming.

The farms near Pompeii were famous throughout the Roman Empire for the wines and olive oils they produced. They also produced plenty of wheat, barley, beans, garlic, and cabbage. Most of the food, clothing, tools, and other necessities required by the owner and his workers were also produced on the farm.

Living quarters were located in rooms along the outer walls. Often the owner and his family lived at one end of the villa and the slaves at the other. In addition to these rooms, the villa had many workrooms, storage rooms, and stables.

many of them were quite elegant.

Immediately inside the front door was the **vestibule**, or entryway, with its altar to the household gods. Beyond the entry was the **atrium**, or front court. The atrium was a large, open square where the master of the house often met clients and guests. The floors were covered with elegant tiles or mosaics, and the walls were usually decorated with colorful **frescoes**, or wall paintings.

The roof above the atrium was supported by rows of columns that formed a square in the middle of the room. Above this square was an opening to let sunlight in. Directly beneath the opening in the roof was a pool to catch the rainwater. The pool was beautifully decorated with mosaics, sculptures, and fountains. The atrium was surrounded by bedrooms, kitchens, libraries, dining rooms, storage rooms, and workrooms.

Large villas and mansions also had a second court called a **peristyle**. The peristyle was usually the largest, most splendid part of the entire house. Like the atrium, it was open in the center, surrounded by small rooms, and often lined with columns. The open area in the peristyle was often used for a garden.

Some of the gardens in Pompeii were spectacular. They had beautiful sculptures, fountains, and even swimming pools. They contained a wonderful variety of flowers and plants. The garden walls were covered with frescoes and mosaics.

CAVE CANEM

### CAVE CANEM

This mosaic is from the porch of a house in Pompeii. The Latin words, Cave Canem, mean "Beware of Dog."

After a long journey, a Roman style bath was just the thing to soothe a weary traveler. Bathing was more than a way to get clean. It was a relaxing pastime practiced daily by people of every age and social rank. Every city had its **thermae**, or public baths, where people would gather in the afternoons and evenings. The *thermae* were usually elegant buildings, and they were often adjoined to sports fields. Before bathing, people enjoyed wrestling, running, swimming, throwing the discus, or doing gymnastics.

Of course, as a guest in one of Pompeii's finer homes, you might enjoy its private baths, complete with hot running water. These baths were usually located in several dome-shaped rooms that were connected by archways. The first room you would come to would be

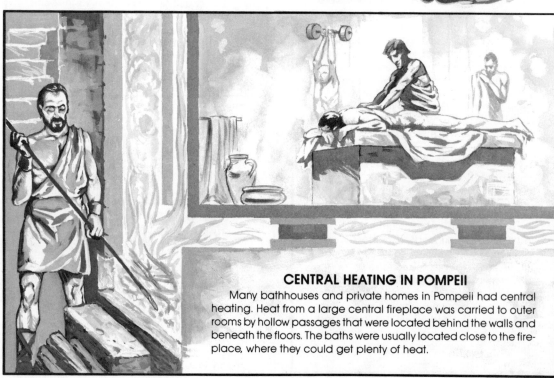

### CENTRAL HEATING IN POMPEII

Many bathhouses and private homes in Pompeii had central heating. Heat from a large central fireplace was carried to outer rooms by hollow passages that were located behind the walls and beneath the floors. The baths were usually located close to the fireplace, where they could get plenty of heat.

the dressing room. Here a slave would help you undress and place your clothes in a brass cupboard. Next you would go to the "warm room" to be massaged by another slave. This slave would rub your body with oil and then use a metal comb to scrape away the dirt.

In the "warm room" were several marble hot tubs. Before soaking in one, however, you would usually enter the "hot room" next door. Here you would sit in a tub of steaming hot water for a few minutes and then return to the "warm room" for a soak in a warm tub. Before dressing for dinner, you might take a brisk swim in the courtyard, or *peristyle*, swimming pool.

## ROMAN ENGINEERING

The people of Pompeii could not enjoy their luxurious baths without a steady supply of running water. So they developed a system for bringing water to Pompeii from a mountain lake 18 miles away (30 kilometers).

The system was not much different from many urban water systems built in the twentieth century. Each day, thousands of gallons of fresh water flowed from the lake to Pompeii through an aqueduct **(1)**. This water was stored in two huge brick reservoirs **(2)**.

The reservoirs were located uphill from Pompeii, so the water could flow downhill through lead pipes to bathhouses, public fountains, public lavatories, and private homes in the city below **(3)**.

In celebration of your visit to Pompeii, your host might have planned a special banquet. This would include music, dancing, wine, and lots of food. At such occasions, men wore their finest cotton or silk togas. Women wore gaily colored *stolas* and showed off their most expensive jewelry.

A slave greeted the guests at the entry to the dining room. "Right foot forward," he reminded them, because it was considered bad luck to enter the dining room with the left foot. As the guests entered, the slave washed their feet and replaced their leather sandals with comfortable slippers.

For a large banquet, couches were often set outdoors in the *peristyle*. As the guests took their assigned places on these couches, they were entertained by slaves, who danced, sang, and played harps and flutes. The entertainment continued throughout the evening.

Exotic dancers swirled around the columns and between the couches. Poets sang the praises of legendary heroes. Magicians dazzled the guests with humorous and amazing tricks.

The seating arrangement at a Roman dinner was important. Each couch held three people, and the couch closest to the serving table was reserved for the host. It was considered a great honor to be seated among the distinguished company near the host. Less important guests sat farther away.

The serving table was covered with a white linen table cloth. A silver bowl, goblet, and knife were set for each guest. Most people brought their own cloth napkins and silver toothpicks. The Romans lay on couches and propped themselves up on one elbow and ate with their fingers.

The food at these banquets was extravagant. Hosts tried to outdo one another, and the result was often a wasteful surplus. For three or four hours, slaves paraded in and out of the *peristyle* with one course of food after another. For appetizers, they served sardines, sea urchins, lobster and other shellfish, nightingales' tongues, and mice rolled in honey and poppy seeds.

Following the appetizers, a procession of slaves usually served six or seven main courses. At a single banquet, guests might be served a bull's eye, a sow's udder stuffed with kidneys, a goose, a lobster, a crab, and huge portions of wild boar!

The roasting of a whole boar was accompanied by great fanfare. Sometimes the animal was decked with the helmet and shield of a foreign enemy. Then a slave, dressed as a Roman soldier, would "attack" the boar and slice it with his sword. Another favorite spectacle was a roast boar stuffed with live birds. When the roast was cut, dozens of birds would fly from its side. It was usually late in the evening before the last of the food was served.

Today when we think of the ancient Romans, we often picture them eating and drinking to excess at these lavish banquets. We should remember, however, that such events were rare, and only a few of the guests ate and drank too much. A more typical evening meal was a quiet affair in the family dining room. With few exceptions (such as breaded mice and nightingales' tongues), most of the food on a Roman table would look familiar to us. Like us, the Romans ate vegetables, fruit, eggs, salads, red meat, poultry, fish, and even ice cream.

# Two
# A Day in the City

Pompeii was enclosed by an enormous wall 20 feet high (6 meters) and 12 feet thick (3.6 meters). The wall was built by the Greeks, who occupied this city for about 500 years before the Romans conquered it. Just beyond the city gates, the streets were lined with small, brick huts. These were not houses but tombs. The Romans built their tombs outside the city because they did not want spirits of the dead roaming their streets at night!

Once inside the city gates, you might be a little disappointed at first. Pompeii was a busy trade city. The sound of carts rattling over the stone roads mingled with the cries of vendors hawking their goods. Some of the carts were pulled by donkeys, others were pulled by slaves.

Most of the streets were so narrow that two carts could barely pass one another. There was not much space between buildings, either, so very little sunlight could shine through. This helped keep the streets cool, but it made them seem dingy and small. They were also filthy because people threw their garbage wherever they pleased. Slaves were supposed to keep the sidewalks and stepping stones clean, but they could not keep up with the mess.

### A ROMAN BAKERY
Pompeii, a city of 20,000 residents, had about forty bakeries. A typical bakery took up a whole house. Of course, that included the mill, where grain was ground into flour.

The grindstones **(1)** for making flour were usually placed in an outdoor court. A grindstone was made of two huge stones, one on top of the other. The top stone was hollow in the center, and it had large wooden handles on two sides. First, grain was poured into the opening on top. Then, as mules or slaves turned the top stone, the grain was ground into flour.

In another room, the flour was mixed into dough, then kneaded and shaped into circular loaves **(2)**. One slave placed the loaves in a big brick oven, and when they were done baking, another slave removed them with an enormous wooden spatula **(3)**. A third slave used an iron "stamp" to label the loaves while they were still hot. Using wheat, barley, millet, and oats, the bakers of Pompeii made at least ten different kinds of bread and one kind of dog biscuit.

By A.D. 79, the streets of Pompeii were overcrowded because business was growing so fast. Many homeowners used parts of their houses for shops, which they managed themselves or rented to others. For this reason, you might see a barber shop, a perfume factory, a tavern, and a fish market all in the same house.

At the fish market, a large window opened toward the street. A horizontal shutter served as a display counter. The names and prices of fish for sale were painted on the wall beside the window. Around the market, an overpowering smell filled the air. It was the smell of **garum**, a spicy sauce made from the entrails of fish. Pompeii was famous for its *garum*. Typically, dozens of people pushed and shoved to get to the fish market window. If you could put up with the crowd, you might enjoy some *garum* for a midday snack, along with a roll from a nearby bakery. In Pompeii, there was always a bakery nearby.

The heart of Pompeii was its forum, and what a contrast it was to the dim, narrow streets of the city. The forum was an open square overlooking the sea. It was surrounded with temples, civic buildings, and statues of emperors, war heroes, and civic leaders. Colorfully-painted rows of columns, or **colonnades**, lined two sides of the square. These columns supported a balcony that was filled with shops and offices.

The forum was the busiest place in town. In fact, the citizens of Pompeii spent most of their time there. Farmers and craftsmen sold their goods at an open market in the center of the forum. Businessmen met their clients there. Lovers often strolled around the colonnade or just stared dreamily out to sea.

School was frequently held at the forum, too. There was no such thing as a school building, so school was held wherever teachers could find a place to meet. Boys, and sometimes girls, began school at age seven. They studied reading, writing, arithmetic, and Greek. The most important subject, though, was **rhetoric**, the art of public speaking. Any young person who wanted to become a leading citizen had to master this skill.

Several of the buildings around the forum were temples honoring Roman gods and goddesses. There were temples of Jupiter, Mars, Apollo, Mercury, Venus, and even Isis, the Egyptian goddess of fertility. As a faithful Roman, you would offer a sacrifice to thank the gods for your safe journey to Pompeii. To do this, you could purchase a live lamb or calf at the forum marketplace and offer it to a priest at one of the temples.

Before A.D. 62, the Temple of Jupiter was the most magnificent temple in

## LAWYERS AND LAWMAKERS

The Roman system of law and justice may have been the greatest achievement of this ancient civilization. Long after the Roman age, modern democratic nations still base their legal systems on the Roman model. Roman lawyers and government leaders were the most respected members of society. Before they could become members of government, however, they had to be wealthy. They were not paid to work for the government. They served because it was a duty and an honor.

In order to get elected, most of them donated large sums of money to their cities. These donations financed the construction of temples and public buildings. Statues of the most generous leaders were erected in the forum alongside the statues of emperors. For a Roman, there could be no greater honor.

Pompeii. It occupied the whole north end of the forum. Then it was struck by a terrible earthquake, which destroyed a large number of buildings in Pompeii. In A.D. 79, the temple was still in ruins. Its roof was collapsed, and a number of its great marble columns lay at the foot of the temple platform.

At the south end of the forum stood

### GOVERNMENT IN POMPEII

The government of Pompeii was modeled after the Roman Senate. It was composed of the city's one hundred most prominent citizens. Instead of being called *senators*, they were called *decurions*. The male citizens of Pompeii elected four *decurions* to serve as the city's chief officers. The two top officials were called **duoviri**. They were like joint mayors. The other two elected officials were called **aediles**, and served as chiefs of police. The *duoviri* and *aediles* served one-year terms, so new elections were held yearly.

the **basilica**, or courthouse, and other city offices. The basilica was a great round building with a domed roof. Inside, as many as four trials could be held at once. In Roman courts such as this, the democratic system of law and justice was born.

Wealthy citizens assigned freedmen and slaves to run their businesses and take care of their homes so that they could spend all their time at the forum. All day these citizens attended trials and listened to political speeches. On a typical day at the forum, they might hear a candidate for city office announce his plan to rebuild the Temple of Jupiter. Another candidate might defend the city's tax plan. Other office seekers tried to buy votes by giving away loaves of bread or sponsoring gladiator games at the local amphitheater. Such bribery was common in Roman politics.

The people of Pompeii loved extravagant shows. They often crowded into one of the city's two theaters to watch plays. On occasion, they used the forum as a circus arena or as a race track for chariot races. But the most popular entertainment of all was the gladiator contest. Like most Roman cities, Pompeii had a gigantic **amphitheater**, or stadium, for these contests. It held 20,000 people, equal to the entire population of the city.

If you attended the games in Pompeii on an afternoon in A.D. 79, you would be joined by people from every walk of life. In the amphitheater, people were seated according to their social rank. The most important citizens had special reserved seats in the front rows. Less prominent citizens had to arrive early to get what good seats were left. Most freedmen and women had to sit near the back, while children and slaves were expected to stand behind them.

The gladiator fights were usually preceded by a wild animal show. Lions, panthers, bears, wolves, and other animals were forced to fight and kill each other. The victorious animals were hunted and killed by soldiers with spears and arrows. This preliminary

## WHO WERE THE GLADIATORS?

Why did these men and women risk their lives for someone else's entertainment? Most of them had no choice. They were either convicted criminals or prisoners captured in war.

Gladiators lived in barracks, which were really more like stables than homes. Still, they were treated better than other prisoners. They were well fed, and they spent most of their time outdoors training for combat.

A few gladiators actually benefited from their careers in the ring. The victors always won prize money, and a few stayed alive long enough to buy their freedom. These successful gladiators became local heroes. Young boys imitated them at play, young women adored them, and graffiti artists praised them. Many of them even became *lanistae*, or owners of gladiators. The *lanistae* benefited more than anyone from these bloody games. They often became rich.

show helped get the crowd into a blood-thirsty mood.

Soon the spectators were in a frenzy. Then an orchestra of trumpets, horns, and flutes blared as the gladiators marched through the arena, displaying their weapons and armor. Occasionally one of them stepped defiantly on a dead animal. Others smeared lion's blood on their arms and faces, hoping this would bring them some of the lion's courage.

Most of the gladiators had bronze helmets and shields, but they carried many different kinds of weapons. Some had long spears, others just had short daggers, while still others held whips and nets. If you looked closely, you would see that a few of these gladiators were women.

After the procession of gladiators, the games were officially dedicated to the spirits of the dead. This custom dated back hundreds of years, to the days when gladiator games first began. At that time, people believed that the spirits demanded human blood, and the gladiator games were a form of religious sacrifice. By the first century A.D. however, the religious dedication was just a ceremony. These games were held strictly for entertainment.

As two gladiators squared off, the crowd waited eagerly for the first blood to be drawn. Spectators booed, cheered, and shouted encouragement to their favorites. They placed bets on who would win. The fact that someone might die did not seem to bother them.

A gladiator contest did not always end in death, however. A gladiator who was wounded but had fought bravely could appeal to the crowd for mercy. The spectators voted by signaling with their

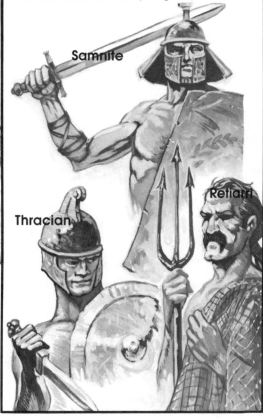

**TYPES OF GLADIATORS**

Different types of gladiators were classified by the weapons and armor they used. Here are three examples: The **Samnite** gladiator was armed with a large shield and sword. A **Thracian** carried only a dagger and a small shield. The **Retiarri** used a fishing net and a **trident**, or three-pronged spear.

hands. Thumbs up was a vote to let the gladiator live, and thumbs down meant he should die. The director of the games surveyed the crowd and then cast the final vote.

The gladiator contests usually lasted several hours, but sometimes they continued for several days! Each contest was a little different. First, a man with a sword might battle a man with a dagger and shield. Next, a man with a whip might take on someone armed with a net and spear. There would be contests between gladiators of different races or nationalities, between two dwarves, two women, or between a man and a woman.

While gladiator games were in progress, the rest of the city was like a ghost town. The forum, usually so full of people, was empty. No priests or worshippers offered sacrifices at the temples. No politicians addressed the crowds. No merchants hawked their wares. No teachers gave lessons, and no beggars begged for food. The only sound was the distant roar of the crowd at the amphitheater. Yet what visitor to this prosperous city in A.D. 79 would have guessed that Pompeii was about to become a real ghost town?

# Three
# The Destruction of Pompeii

In A.D. 79, Pompeii must have seemed like a wonderful place to live. Its stately forum and elegant mansions were signs of its peace and prosperity. For several years, however, there had been disturbing signals from Mt. Vesuvius that something was wrong.

The first signal came in A.D. 62, when a great earthquake destroyed many buildings in Pompeii, including the Temple of Jupiter. The earthquake was caused by pressure from the melted rock, or **magma**, that was building up beneath the volcano.

The people of Pompeii had no idea that the earthquake was a signal of future danger. After all, Vesuvius had not erupted for centuries. They had heard the old legends about fire-breathing monsters inside the mountain and giants hurling fire into the air. There was even a blackened crater at the top of the mountain, but that did not seem to be cause for alarm. People just planted

## WHAT IS A VOLCANO?

The earth's surface, or **crust**, is made of rock. It is about 50 miles thick (80 kilometers), but it is divided into several huge pieces, called **plates**. As these plates bump and rub together, the friction melts some of the rock. The melted rock, or **magma**, rises toward the surface through gaps and weak spots in the earth's crust. These gaps are called **vents**.

A **volcano** is the place where a vent reaches the surface. If the magma is thin enough to flow out of the volcano, a **lava eruption** occurs. Over thousands of years, the hardened lava that builds up around the volcano forms a mountain, or **cone**.

If the magma is too thick to flow as lava, it remains trapped beneath the earth's surface. Then the pressure from explosive gases builds and builds until the magma explodes. The explosion may have enough force to blow the top of a mountain to bits. Such eruptions are called **Plinian eruptions**.

In a Plinian eruption, the magma is blown high into the air as a foamy liquid. Before falling to the ground, the liquid hardens into light-weight stones full of air holes. These stones are called **pumice**.

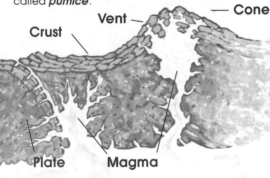

This 1985 eruption of Mt. St. Helens in Washington State is a recent example of a Plinian eruption.

grapevines in the rich soil of the crater.

After the earthquake, the residents of Pompeii wanted to make their city more beautiful than ever. They rebuilt damaged houses and public buildings and added new ones. Some people even built new mountainside villas right at the edge of the crater.

By A.D. 79, people had begun to notice other disturbing signs near Mt. Vesuvius. For one thing, wells and springs were drying up. In early August, the ground began to rumble and shake. A series of small earthquakes cracked a few walls and broke a few windows, but caused no major damage.

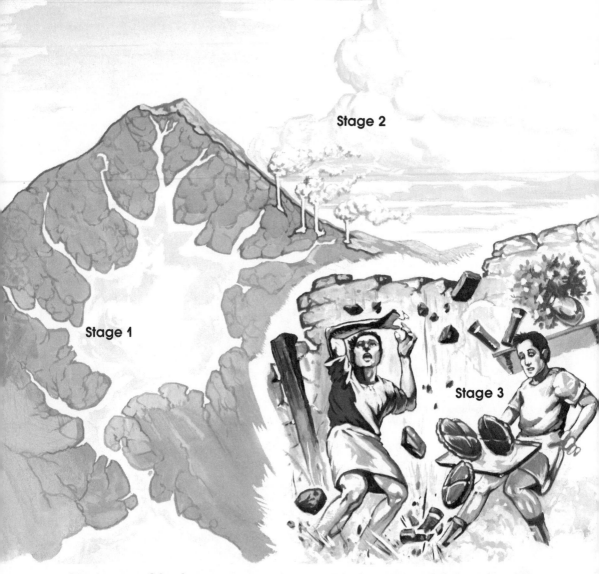

Stage 2

Stage 1

Stage 3

On August 20, there was greater rumbling and shaking. Giant spouts of steam shot up from the normally calm bay. Birds and other wild animals, probably sensing that something terrible was about to happen, fled from the mountain.

About half the residents of Pompeii did the same. However, many slaves and poor people stayed behind because they had nowhere else to go. And a number of wealthy citizens stayed because they did not want to leave their comfort-able homes and valuable possessions. Besides, most of them had survived the earthquake of A.D. 62, and they believed that they could survive another. Of course, they did not know what was coming.

On the morning of August 24, a series of steam explosions burst through the floor of the crater at the top of Mt. Vesuvius. Then, at about 1:30 P.M. the mountain was rocked by a tremendous blast. The crater split open, and the top of the mountain was blown to bits. A

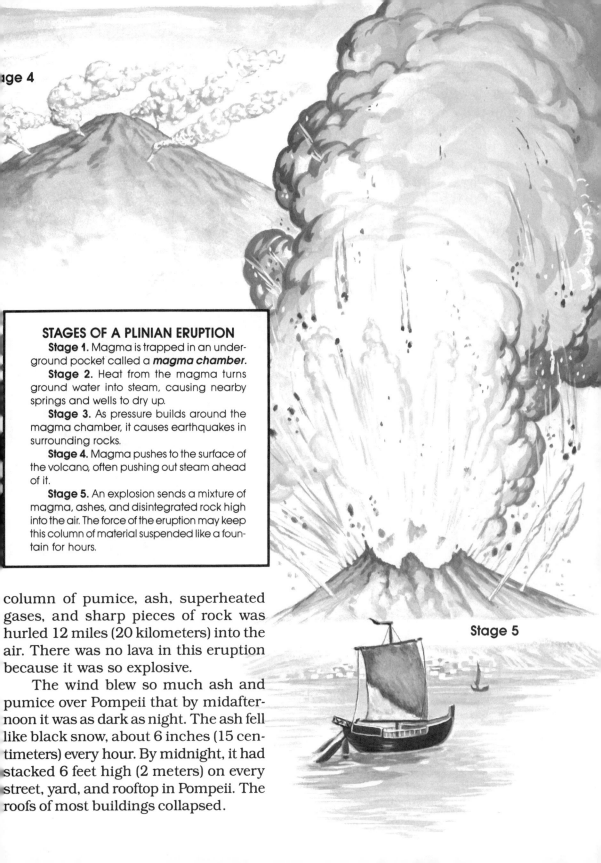

**STAGES OF A PLINIAN ERUPTION**

**Stage 1.** Magma is trapped in an underground pocket called a *magma chamber.*

**Stage 2.** Heat from the magma turns ground water into steam, causing nearby springs and wells to dry up.

**Stage 3.** As pressure builds around the magma chamber, it causes earthquakes in surrounding rocks.

**Stage 4.** Magma pushes to the surface of the volcano, often pushing out steam ahead of it.

**Stage 5.** An explosion sends a mixture of magma, ashes, and disintegrated rock high into the air. The force of the eruption may keep this column of material suspended like a fountain for hours.

**Stage 5**

column of pumice, ash, superheated gases, and sharp pieces of rock was hurled 12 miles (20 kilometers) into the air. There was no lava in this eruption because it was so explosive.

The wind blew so much ash and pumice over Pompeii that by midafternoon it was as dark as night. The ash fell like black snow, about 6 inches (15 centimeters) every hour. By midnight, it had stacked 6 feet high (2 meters) on every street, yard, and rooftop in Pompeii. The roofs of most buildings collapsed.

Around midnight on August 24, the first *glowing avalanche* rolled down Mt. Vesuvius. It did not reach Pompeii, but on the north side of the mountain, it struck the beautiful resort city of **Herculaneum**, killing everyone there. Because Herculaneum was closer than Pompeii to the eruption, it was buried more deeply by the glowing avalanches. The following morning, two more avalanches burst through Herculaneum, but once again, Pompeii was spared.

All this time, however, ash and pumice continued to fall on the city of Pompeii. In all, about 20 feet (6 meters) of this material fell on the city, trapping people inside their homes or beneath collapsed buildings. Most people, though, escaped to the roofs, balconies, and second stories that remained standing above the ash and rubble.

Then came the fourth avalanche — the first three glowing avalanches had stopped before they reached Pompeii. But sometime on the morning of August 25, the surge from the fourth avalanche

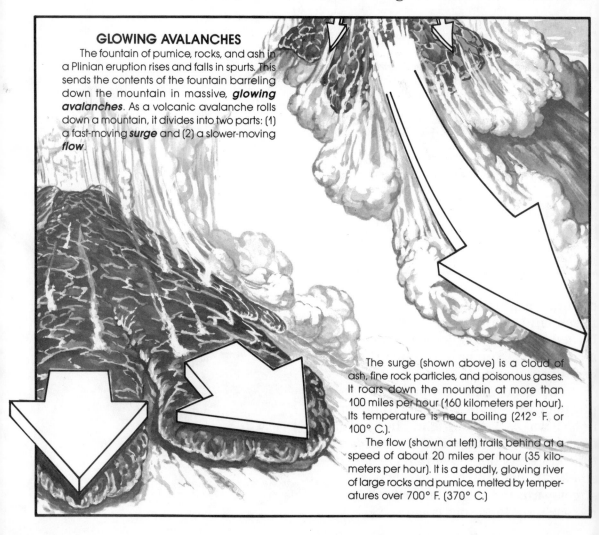

**GLOWING AVALANCHES**

The fountain of pumice, rocks, and ash in a Plinian eruption rises and falls in spurts. This sends the contents of the fountain barreling down the mountain in massive, *glowing avalanches*. As a volcanic avalanche rolls down a mountain, it divides into two parts: (1) a fast-moving *surge* and (2) a slower-moving *flow*.

The surge (shown above) is a cloud of ash, fine rock particles, and poisonous gases. It roars down the mountain at more than 100 miles per hour (160 kilometers per hour). Its temperature is near boiling (212° F. or 100° C.).

The flow (shown at left) trails behind at a speed of about 20 miles per hour (35 kilometers per hour). It is a deadly, glowing river of large rocks and pumice, melted by temperatures over 700° F. (370° C.)

rushed over the walls and through the gates of the city. Within minutes, everyone who was still alive was killed. The dense cloud of ash blasted through Pompeii like a blinding sandstorm and knocked people off their feet. The ash and toxic gases in the cloud filled their noses, throats, and lungs. They suffocated moments before the superheated flow followed the surge into the city and buried everything in its path.

In these horrifying final hours, Pompeii was transformed. This once-prosperous city of pleasure, this jewel of the Roman Empire, had become a graveyard. On August 25 and 26, at least two more avalanches buried the city even more deeply before Mt. Vesuvius finally grew quiet.

After the eruption, the air was filled with the sickening smell of sulphur. Where beautiful pine trees and lush meadows had once adorned the countryside, the land was now bare. A thick layer of gray ash covered the ground where beautiful villas once stood. Blackened pumice stones lay scattered everywhere.

Mt. Vesuvius looked as if something had swallowed its top half and taken a huge bite from its side. The slopes, which had once been thick with trees and vineyards, were now black and bare. There were no signs of Pompeii: no roads, no houses, no walls, not even fragments or ruins of walls.

because they describe the death of his uncle, Pliny the Elder, who was killed during the eruption. Pliny the Elder was a pioneer of science. His study of nature, entitled *Natural History*, is one of the finest scientific works of the ancient world.

When the eruption of Mt. Vesuvius began, Pliny the Elder was commanding a fleet of Roman ships stationed at Misenum. From there, he and his nephew could see the enormous cloud of ash, rocks, and smoke that blasted 12 miles (20 kilometers) into the sky. Being a scientist, Pliny the Elder decided to sail closer so that he could get a better view.

Instead of going with his uncle, Pliny the Younger decided to stay in Misenum to look after his mother. From there, he had an excellent view of the ash cloud rising over Mt. Vesuvius, as he describes in his letter to Tacitus:

*The shape and appearance of that cloud was like a pine tree. Rising into the air like an immense tree trunk, it opened out into branches. It scattered widely, part white, part dark and flecked, according to the amount of earth or ashes it carried.*

People in nearby cities and towns told fantastic stories about what had happened. Some claimed that they saw giants standing on the fiery mountain and hurling rocks at the cities below. Others said that Vulcanus, the Roman god of the underworld, had been so angry that he broke the mountain open and threw out fire and rocks. Almost everyone agreed that some god must have been very angry, for they had never seen such destruction before.

To the people of that age, these explanations made sense. After all, they did not understand what volcanoes were, and most of them did not think scientifically. One exception was the writer Pliny the Younger. He witnessed the eruption from the town of Misenum, about 20 miles (32 kilometers) from Mt. Vesuvius. Pliny attempted to describe the event as accurately as he could. His personal letters to the famous Roman historian, Tacitus, contain one of the world's oldest eyewitness accounts of a natural disaster.

Pliny's letters are extremely moving

Meanwhile, Pliny the Elder had given orders to prepare a small boat for sailing toward Mt. Vesuvius. Before departing, however, he received a message from Rectina, the wife of a close friend who lived at the foot of Mt. Vesuvius. From there, her only hope of escape was by ship. As his nephew's letter shows, Pliny the Elder made a heroic decision:

*Pliny the Elder decided to take a larger ship so that he could rescue Rectina and her neighbors. He steered eastwards, straight into the danger. Already, ashes were falling on the boat. These became hotter and thicker as the boat drew nearer to Vesuvius.*

*Also, pumice-stones and sharp, black spears of shattered rock fell around them. The sea was driven back by rubble from the mountain, and the shore was unreachable. For a moment, my uncle considered turning back, and his pilot urged him to do so.*

Pliny, however, thought of another old friend, Pomponianus, who lived in the city of Stabiae. This city was also in grave danger, but he believed they could still reach it:

*Fortune favors the brave, he said then. "Make for Pomponianus."*

A strong wind guided Pliny's ship into port at Stabiae. He found Pomponianus at home. His friend was frightened and wanted to leave immediately, but the wind was too strong to sail against. Pliny did his best to comfort him:

Pomponianus was frightened and upset, but Pliny embraced and cheered and encouraged him. To reassure him with his own self-confidence, he went to bathe. After that he sat down and ate with gusto.

However, at several places on Mt. Vesuvius, great flames could be seen in the night. To calm his companions' fears, my uncle told them that the flames were probably from campfires built by farmers who had fled from their mountain homes. Then he lay down and slept a proper sleep, for those who stayed near the door heard him snore.

While Pliny the Elder slept, ash and pumice from the volcano continued to fall. Soon it began to fill the courtyards at Pomponianus's home. Pliny awoke and went to discuss the situation with Pomponianus and the others:

They could do nothing but wait for the wind to shift. So Pliny the Elder lay down on a blanket to rest. Perhaps he already suspected that this was to be his final resting place:

*Should they stay in the house or flee to the country? By this time, the house was shaken by frequent tremors. As if torn from its foundation, it tilted right and left. In the open, there was the danger of the falling pumice-stones, though these were charred and light.*

*They chose to flee. With towels, they tied pillows to their heads to protect them from the falling stones. In the streets, people carried torches and lights of every kind. It was early morning, but still as dark as the blackest and thickest night. They made their way back to the shore, hoping that the sea would be calm enough to sail, but it was still too wild.*

*Twice he called for cold water and drank it. Soon the flames and the odor of poisonous gases forced my uncle to get up. Leaning on two young slaves, he rose and immediately fell down dead. I suppose that the thick smoke must have choked him, since his lungs were naturally weak.*

*When light returned to Stabiae three days later, his body was found without any noticeable injury, and his clothing was not disturbed in the least. He looked more like a man asleep than like a dead one.*

In a second letter to Tacitus, Pliny the Younger describes his own harrowing experience at Misenum:

*It was the first hour after sunrise, but the light was still faint. The buildings around us were shaking so much that they seemed certain to collapse. My mother and I decided to get out of town. The panic-stricken crowds followed us, because they did not know what else to do. The huge throng of frightened people harassed and jostled us.*

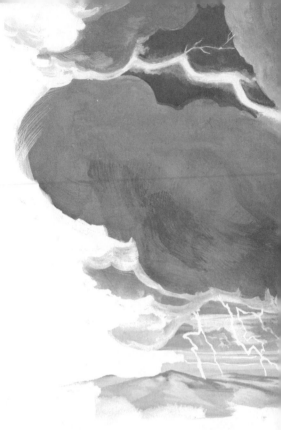

The earth shook so hard that Pliny could barely steer their chariot. The tremors had caused the sea to recede, stranding thousands of sea creatures on the sand. Looking toward the mountain, he saw a terrible black cloud torn by streaks of volcanic lightning.

Then the ash began to fall, sparsely at first, but gradually becoming heavier until they were surrounded by total darkness. Thick smoke filled the air and made breathing difficult. The eerie silence was broken only by the crying and shouting of children and parents who had become separated. To Pliny the Younger, it must have seemed as if the whole world was coming to an end:

*Then a faint light appeared to us. We thought it was a sign of the approaching fire, but it disappeared some distance from us. Once more, we were surrounded by darkness and ashes, now thick and heavy. From time to time we had to get up and shake them off for fear of being actually buried and crushed under their weight. I imagined that one with all and all with one were going to die.*

Suddenly, the darkness began to fade. When daylight finally returned, however, Misenum and the surrounding countryside had changed dramatically:

*Finally, a genuine daylight came, the sun even shone, but dimly, as in an eclipse. And then everything appeared changed and covered, as by an abundant snowfall, with a thick layer of ashes.*

Scientists today still marvel at Pliny's precise description of an explosive volcanic eruption, which they often call a Plinian eruption. In addition, Pliny's eye-witness account lets us sense the terror and the drama of this historic event. Without these letters, much of what happened to Pompeii and to the other cities on Mt. Vesuvius might never have been known.

## Four

# The Lost City Comes to Life

After the eruption, people returned to the place where Pompeii had been. Some scraped and dug through the rubble for their belongings. Others looked for signs of their lost families and homes. All they found were a few broken bricks and roof tiles. Eventually, they just gave up.

They settled in other cities and began new lives. As time went by, people told their children, grandchildren, and great-grandchildren about the beautiful city that had been destroyed. But as generations passed, the name Pompeii was forgotten, and people merely referred to it as the "lost city" near Mt. Vesuvius.

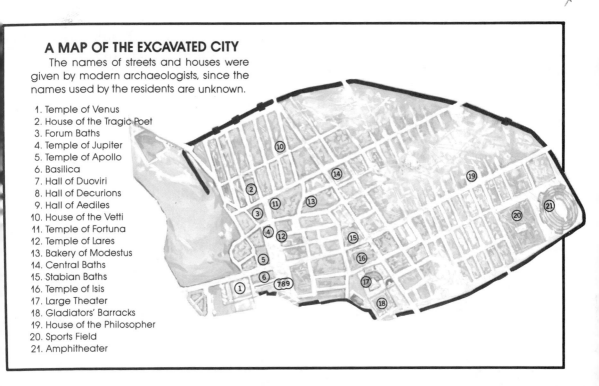

## A MAP OF THE EXCAVATED CITY

The names of streets and houses were given by modern archaeologists, since the names used by the residents are unknown.

1. Temple of Venus
2. House of the Tragic Poet
3. Forum Baths
4. Temple of Jupiter
5. Temple of Apollo
6. Basilica
7. Hall of Duoviri
8. Hall of Decurions
9. Hall of Aediles
10. House of the Vetti
11. Temple of Fortuna
12. Temple of Lares
13. Bakery of Modestus
14. Central Baths
15. Stabian Baths
16. Temple of Isis
17. Large Theater
18. Gladiators' Barracks
19. House of the Philosopher
20. Sports Field
21. Amphitheater

Hundreds of years went by, and the Roman Empire came to an end. Most of it was conquered by barbarians from the north. They were primitive people who had no use for Roman law, art, and learning. Roman civilization was all but forgotten. Only ruined buildings and a number of scrolls and letters remained from this once-great civilization.

Then in 1709, a remarkable discovery shocked the world. An Italian workman was digging a well on the slopes of Mt. Vesuvius, and he dug right into an ancient Roman theater! After three more years of digging, workers finally hollowed out the inside of this ancient building. It was identified as the theater at Herculaneum. It must have looked then just like it did on the day of the eruption in A.D. 79.

We will never be certain, though, because the excavators took most of the valuable art, sculptures, and other furnishings out of the theater. Nevertheless, the discovery of Herculaneum renewed interest in the lost cities of Vesuvius.

Historians began to wonder what had happened to Pompeii. For forty years, people combed the mountainsides looking for clues. Then in 1748, the Spanish engineer Roque de Alcubierre discovered a temple that had been part of the forum in Pompeii. Thus began one of the greatest stories in the history of archaeology.

Unfortunately, archaeology was a very new science in those days. In fact, it was more like a big treasure hunt than a science. Many of the excavators were more interested in profit than in history. They sold most of what they found to museums and private collectors. We will never know what was inside those first buildings discovered in Pompeii.

In 1861, the archaeologist Giuseppi Fiorelli became the director of excavations at Pompeii, and he put a stop to the treasure hunts. Fiorelli realized how much Pompeii could teach us about the Roman Empire. So he developed scientific methods for excavating the city. By studying the buildings, artifacts, and corpses, Fiorelli and later archaeologists have gradually put together an accurate picture of Pompeii before the eruption.

Clearing away the ash and rock from the streets and buildings, they found sculptures, paintings, mosaics, furniture, tools, dishes, jewelry, and other artifacts from everyday life. Like a gigantic jigsaw puzzle, they have put Pompeii back together as they think it actually looked two thousand years ago.

When you visit Pompeii today, you feel as though you are spying on the people who once lived there. At a bakery that belonged to a man named Modestus, eighty-one loaves of bread, nearly 2,000

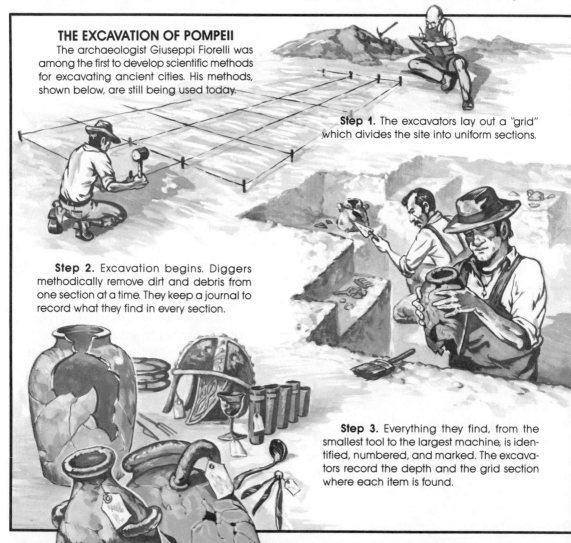

## THE EXCAVATION OF POMPEII
The archaeologist Giuseppi Fiorelli was among the first to develop scientific methods for excavating ancient cities. His methods, shown below, are still being used today.

**Step 1.** The excavators lay out a "grid" which divides the site into uniform sections.

**Step 2.** Excavation begins. Diggers methodically remove dirt and debris from one section at a time. They keep a journal to record what they find in every section.

**Step 3.** Everything they find, from the smallest tool to the largest machine, is identified, numbered, and marked. The excavators record the depth and the grid section where each item is found.

years old, are still sitting in the oven. Frescoes in a tailor shop belonging to a man named Ubonius show all the steps for dyeing wool. And the vats for doing this important job still stand in the shop, ready to use. At a house that archaeologists call the House of the Philosopher, the master must have been expecting guests. His dining room table is still set with silver cups and a full jug of wine.

The home of the Vetti family was one of the largest and finest houses in all of Pompeii. Today it is restored so accurately that visitors almost expect to bump into members of the family. The bronze front doors stand open, as if permitting guests to enter without disturbing the doorman. The altar in the entryway is so well preserved that visitors still place flowers, wine, incense, or other gifts on it for the household gods. Cupboards in the atrium are still filled with silver cups, platters, and candleholders used by the Vettis for entertaining guests. Mosaics, sculptures, and colorful frescoes decorate the walls.

In the middle of the *peristyle*, the Vetti's splendid garden has also been restored. Stately columns and graceful statues remind us of the grandeur of Roman architecture. Running water flowing from fountains reminds us of the genius of Roman engineering. Roses, violets, hyacinths, and other beautiful plants grow along the colonnade. Researchers tell us that these are exactly the same plants that the Vetti family grew.

**Step 4.** Scientists treat the artifacts with a protective coating. They study the artifacts carefully before returning them to the buildings where they were found. Using the knowledge they have gained, archaeologists have tried to make Pompeii look just like it did in A.D. 79.

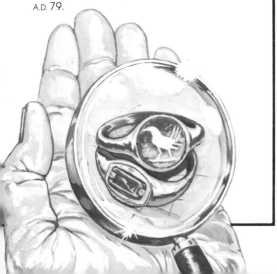

The restored peristyle, or courtyard, of the Vetti House as it appears today.

Besides finding buildings that are 2,000 years old, the excavators of Pompeii often find themselves face to face with 2,000-year-old skeletons! These belonged to the victims who were buried under the loosely packed ash and pumice that fell like snow on Pompeii. Today, only fragments of the skeletons remain.

Other victims have been preserved in a more incredible way. People who managed to climb above the ash and pumice were killed when the surge from a glowing avalanche reached the city on the morning of August 25, A.D. 79. The moist ash from this surge did an amazing thing. It packed gently around the victims' bodies and insulated them against the hot flow of molten rock that followed. Although this insulation did not save the victims' lives, it did form perfect molds around their bodies. And 1,800 years later, archaeologist Giuseppi Fiorelli invented a way to make plaster casts from these molds.

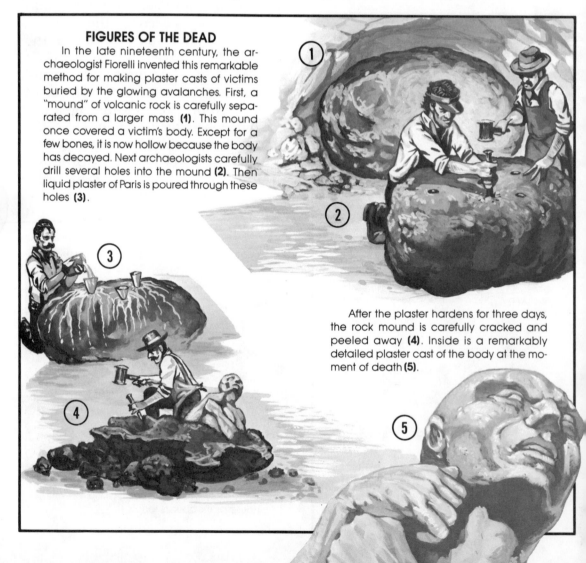

### FIGURES OF THE DEAD

In the late nineteenth century, the archaeologist Fiorelli invented this remarkable method for making plaster casts of victims buried by the glowing avalanches. First, a "mound" of volcanic rock is carefully separated from a larger mass (1). This mound once covered a victim's body. Except for a few bones, it is now hollow because the body has decayed. Next archaeologists carefully drill several holes into the mound (2). Then liquid plaster of Paris is poured through these holes (3).

After the plaster hardens for three days, the rock mound is carefully cracked and peeled away (4). Inside is a remarkably detailed plaster cast of the body at the moment of death (5).

The plaster casts transform hollow lumps of volcanic rock into life-like figures of the victims at the moment they died. Many of the casts show minute details, such as bumps and moles on the skin. They reveal what kind of clothes the victims wore (complete with folds and wrinkles), their sex, their hairstyles, and even their facial expressions. With the help of these remarkable casts, it is possible to picture the final hours.

On the afternoon of August 24, the streets were almost pitch dark. The only light came from the ghostly glow of Mt. Vesuvius. People ran madly in every direction. They covered their heads with pillows, plates, kettles, and anything else they could grab. Some probably thought it safest to run indoors, while others fled to the countryside.

In the confusion, families became separated. Parents and children called to one another, but with all the shouting and commotion, no one could be understood. There were probably heavily armed gladiators in the crowd, swinging their fists and swords, knocking down anyone who got in their way.

heavy bag of coins in one hand and a sword in the other. The mistress of a large mansion was discovered in front of her house with three of her maids. Strewn around them were coins, jewels, and a silver mirror.

Another richly dressed woman, wearing magnificent jewelry, died in the gladiator barracks — a rather unusual place for a woman of her class. We do not know exactly what she was doing there, but many wealthy women in Pompeii secretly enjoyed the company of strong, handsome gladiators.

One woman, with a baby in her arms, fell while running toward a city gate. Beside her, clutching at her dress, were two little girls. Apparently, the woman was trying to get these children out of the city.

Even if they had made it through the gate, they would not have been safer in the country. Only a few villas outside of Pompeii were ever found. As far as we know, no one was in them at the time of the eruption. Judging from the number of bodies found just outside the gates, however, and the positions they were facing, many people must have been trying to get into the city.

Among them were a young woman and a small boy, probably her son. When the weight of the wet ash forced them to the ground, the woman wrapped her body around the boy, trying in vain to protect him. Nearby lay two other little boys, perhaps brothers, holding hands.

Other victims tried to save whatever they could. One man was found with a

## FACING FATE

One street in Pompeii contained so many bodies that archaeologists call it "Skeleton Alley."

Among the victims found on this street was a group of three people: two well-dressed women, probably a mother and daughter, and a large, muscular man who was probably their slave. What is remarkable about these three figures is how differently each of them reacted to certain death.

The "daughter" is sprawled on the ground with outstretched arms and clenched fists. Her face is full of anguish. The "slave" shows the frustration of a strong man whose strength could not save him. The plaster cast of his body preserves his last, futile effort to lift himself up against the heavy ash. Beside these two figures, the "mother" lay serenely on her side with her head on her arms, as if sleeping peacefully.

Judging by their clothing, many of the victims were slaves and beggars. They, too, grabbed whatever meager possessions they could. One half-naked man held a small cloth bag that was nearly empty, except for a few small coins and a pair of sandals. Another man, probably a poor farmer, was found holding a goat by its collar. Why this man was trying to drag the animal with him, we will never know.

Some victims left a trail of clues behind. Archaeologists have pieced these clues together, like detectives solving a mystery. Consider the case of the priests at the Temple of Isis.

As a glowing avalanche began rolling toward the city, this group of priests was sharing a meal in the temple. Two thousand years later, the charred eggs and fish from their meal can still be seen on the table where they had been seated! When the priests saw the surge cloud coming, they must have gathered all the statues, gold and silver plates, and other valuables that they could carry, and ran out of the temple.

They struggled through the deep ash and pumice. A priest carrying a heavy sack full of valuables was the first to fall. Moments later, several of his companions were killed when a row of columns fell on them. Alongside their bodies, archaeologists have discovered a statue of Isis, a silver plaque, an Egyptian musical instrument, and a magnificent silver water bowl.

The other priests sought shelter in

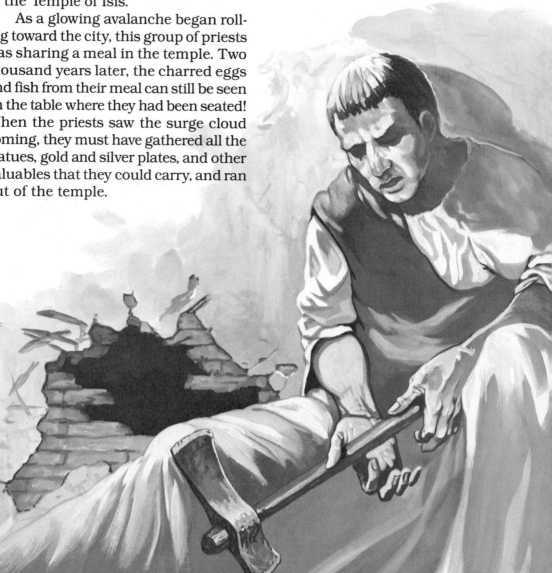

a nearby house. Here the surge cloud caught up with them. The last to die was a priest who had found a hatchet and had chopped through several walls trying to escape. He was found leaning against a wall, still holding the hatchet in his hands.

Finally, a series of clues in one of Pompeii's mansions tell the story of a loyal and loving father. Based on tablets found in the house, archaeologists believe the man's name was Erotus. He was the steward, or head slave, in this house. His master had fled from Pompeii before the eruption began and left Erotus in charge.

After the eruption, ash and pumice piled so high around the house that the doors and windows were blocked. The

other slaves in the house tried to escape through the second story windows. But it was too late. Ten of them were trapped on the stairway, and the rest were trapped on the roof.

Erotus did not try to escape. With his small daughter by his side, he stayed at his post near the entryway. There he made the girl lie down on his bed, and he covered her with pillows. He sat next to her, clutching the purse and the wax seal that his master had left in his care. This is how Erotus and his daughter were found, 1,800 years later.

Today, more than one hundred years after archaeologist Giuseppi Fiorelli began his work there, nearly one-third of Pompeii and two-thirds of Herculaneum remain buried. Nearby villages have never been found. Who knows what treasures, secrets, and mysteries still lie hidden in the lost cities of Vesuvius?

---

## THE PHASES OF DEATH

As many as 10,000 people may have been in Pompeii when Mt. Vesuvius erupted on August 24, A.D. 79. But they were not all killed instantly. Although people died in many different ways, there were three quite distinct phases:

**STAGE 1:** The first people to die in Pompeii were struck by sharp, flying rocks, or crushed beneath collapsing roofs and columns while trying to flee from the city.

**STAGE 2:** As the ash continued to fall, it blocked windows and doorways in all the buildings. Hundreds of residents were trapped inside their homes, where they were buried under the ash and suffocated.

**STAGE 3:** Most people in Pompeii stayed above the ashfall by climbing up stairs and onto balconies and rooftops. They were still alive on August 25, when the glowing avalanche hit Pompeii. Then the surge of pumice, ash, and poisonous gases swept through the entire city. Almost instantly, everyone who was still alive suffocated. The moist ash, however, protected their bodies, so they were not burned up by the molten rock that covered them moments later.

## Five

# Living with the Volcano

Mt. Vesuvius has erupted 18 times since A.D. 79. The last time was in 1944, but this was mild compared to earlier eruptions. For example, a single volcanic eruption in 1631 killed more than 10,000 people. Afterwards, the Viceroy of Naples erected a sign at the foot of Mt. Vesuvius with this warning:

*Children and children's children, hear! In the heart of this mountain is stored much evil. Sooner or later it will take fire. Flee as quickly as you can.*

Despite such warnings, people still choose to live on this murderous mountain. For the past 2,000 years, whenever Mt. Vesuvius has been quiet, people have built their homes on its beautiful slopes. Today, more than 70,000 people live right on the mountain.

Recently, there have been a number of terrible earthquakes near Mt. Vesuvius. In 1980, an earthquake killed 3,000 people in Naples and left more than 100,000 homeless. These earthquakes are caused by magma moving beneath the volcano. Scientists say they are a sign that a volcanic eruption is coming.

Some people seem to welcome the challenge of living next to an active volcano. Consider the residents of San Sebastiano, a small town located just three miles below the main crater of Mt. Vesuvius. Nearly every generation of residents in San Sebastiano has seen the volcano's destructive power.

During the eruption of 1944, the entire town had to be evacuated, and two-thirds of it was destroyed. Instead of abandoning their city after the eruption, the people of San Sebastiano returned. In defiance of Vesuvius, they repaired old buildings and put up new ones. They even built right on top of the new lava flows.

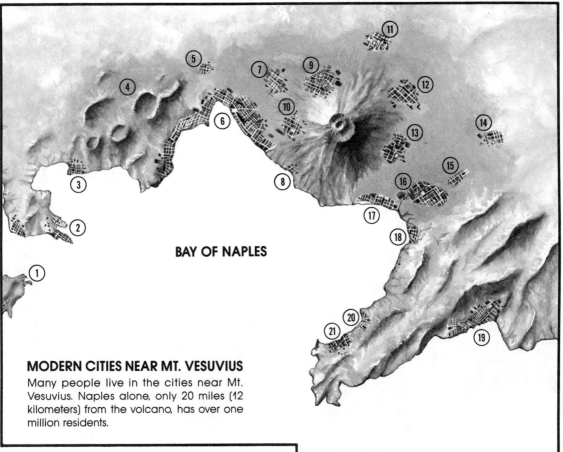

**BAY OF NAPLES**

## MODERN CITIES NEAR MT. VESUVIUS

Many people live in the cities near Mt. Vesuvius. Naples alone, only 20 miles (12 kilometers) from the volcano, has over one million residents.

1. Procida
2. Miseno (Misenum)
3. Pozzuoli (Puteoli)
4. Phlegrean Fields
5. Frattsumaggiore
6. Naples
7. Afragala
8. Ercolano (Herculaneum)
9. Pomigliano
10. San Sebastiano
11. Nola
12. San Giuseppe (Vesuviano)
13. Terzigno
14. Poggiomarino
15. Scafati
16. Pompei (Pompeii)
17. Torre Annunziata (Oplontis)
18. Castellmmare di Stabia (Stabiae)
19. Positano
20. Meta
21. Sorrento (Sarrentum)

## MT. VESUVIUS AS IT LOOKS TODAY

Mt. Vesuvius looks different now than it did in A.D. 79. Today there are two peaks instead of one. The taller of the two is called Mt. Vesuvius, and the other is Mt. Somma. Mt. Somma is actually the older peak.

In Roman times, this "old" Mt. Vesuvius was a lone peak towering 6,000 feet above sea level (1,800 meters). During the eruption of A.D. 79, half of it was destroyed, and a huge crater was formed on its northern slope. Out of this crater, the "new" Mt. Vesuvius has been growing with each eruption. It is a volcanic cone that now reaches 4,000 feet above sea level (1,200 meters). Future lava eruptions could add to its height, unless of course, another Plinian eruption causes the cone to explode.

After Mt. Vesuvius erupts, people often rebuild right over the new lava flows.

Why do these people keep coming back when they know that an eruption or earthquake will probably destroy their city again? Are they foolish or courageous? We cannot say, but we can understand why they are so attached to their homes. In many cases, their families have lived and worked here for several generations. Many residents of San Sebastiano live in homes that were restored after previous eruptions.

Besides, San Sebastiano has many of the same features that made Pompeii so popular in Roman times. Attracted by the fresh mountain air, the scenic countryside, and the Mediterranean climate, more people settle in this town all the time. Before the eruption in 1944, only 4,000 people lived here. Today, San Sebastiano is a thriving community of 8,000 residents.

As Rafael Capasso, mayor of San Sebastiano for more than twenty years, said,

> *This city is proof that the power of the human spirit is stronger than the power of the volcano.*

Is Mayor Capasso right? Will San Sebastiano endure in spite of the dangers of Mt. Vesuvius? Or will archaeologists 2,000 years from now be trying to piece together the final, horrifying hours of this once-beautiful city?

No one can predict exactly when the next eruption will occur, but every year on September 19, thousands of people gather at the old Cathedral of Naples, hoping for a clue. This is the feast day of Saint Gennaro, the patron saint of Naples. Many Roman Catholics believe that St. Gennaro protects the region from the evils of Mt. Vesuvius. He signals his promise of protection with a miracle on his feast day. If this miracle takes place, the faithful believe that they will be kept safe from earthquakes and eruptions for another year.

### THE MIRACLE OF ST. GENNARO

An enormous old cathedral stands in the heart of Naples. Each year on September 19, thousands of people crowd into the cathedral to celebrate the feast day of Saint Gennaro, the patron saint of Naples. Roman Catholics believe that he protects them from earthquakes and other natural disasters.

A vessel containing some of Gennaro's dried blood is kept in the cathedral. On his feast day, the vessel is brought to the altar, and usually the dried blood miraculously turns to liquid. The faithful believe that this is a promise from St. Gennaro to protect the region from the evil powers of Vesuvius for another year.

Sometimes the dried blood does not turn to liquid. The last time this happened was in 1979. The following year, a great earthquake struck Naples, killing 3,000 people and leaving 100,000 homeless.

The Roman Catholic Church has never allowed anyone to examine St. Gennaro's blood. Therefore, scientists cannot explain how it turns to liquid. However, most of them doubt that it has any effect on Mt. Vesuvius.

Rather than wait for a miracle, **volcanologists** (scientists who study volcanoes) come from around the world to study at the Mt. Vesuvius Observatory. By examining the data that have been collected there, they have identified a two-or-three thousand year cycle with three distinct phases of activity.

The first phase, the Plinian eruption, is the most violent. Plinian eruptions occur only once every 2,000 or 3,000 years, and the last one destroyed Pompeii in A.D. 79. This phase is followed by a "mixed eruption" phase. A mixed eruption is a combination of explosive activity and lava flows. These usually occur about once every hundred years, and the phase lasts at least 1,000 years. Although they are not as explosive as Plinian eruptions, mixed eruptions can still be extremely destructive. The last one, in 1631, killed 10,000 people.

The third phase is a series of "mild eruptions" that occur about every fifty years. Mt. Vesuvius is now in the third phase, but it has not erupted in over half a century. This could mean that another mild eruption will occur soon. It could also mean that this phase is ending and the volcano is building toward another Plinian eruption. As time passes, a violent eruption becomes more likely. As one volcanologist put it:

> *Minor volcanic activity helps vent eruptive force. When the cork finally does come out of the bottle, the sudden release of gases accumulated over the last fifty years could lead to a particularly violent eruption.*

An eruption today like the one in A.D. 79 could kill thousands of people. That is why accurate predictions are important. Scientists at the Mt. Vesuvius Observatory use an array of instruments to monitor the mountain 24 hours a day. They watch for signs that Mt. Vesuvius is getting ready to erupt.

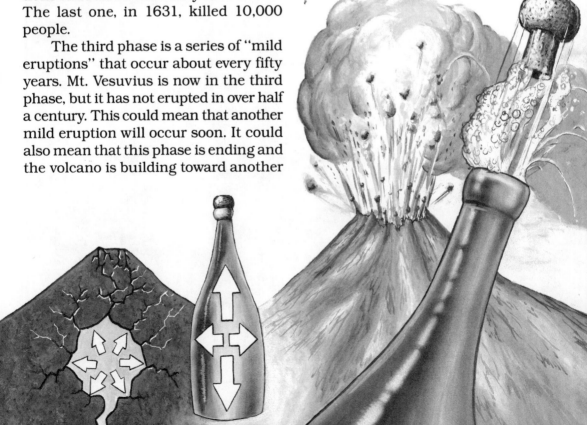

## WATCHING THE SLEEPING GIANT

A **seismograph** is a machine that measures vibrations of the earth's surface. It can detect even the slightest tremble. By charting all the vibrations in a volcanic region, experts can locate magma chambers. As a magma chamber grows, it causes the land above it to vibrate. That is why a sudden increase in earthquake activity is a sign that an eruption is coming.

The movement of magma beneath the earth's surface also causes the land to rise or sink. Electronic **tiltmeters** detect even the slightest changes in the shape of the land.

Heat from magma turns ground water to steam. Scientists keep a constant eye on the level and temperature of ground water in nearby wells and springs.

Changes can often be detected at sea before they can be detected on land. That is why volcanologists at the Mt. Vesuvius Observatory have placed thermometers, water level gauges, seismographs, and tiltmeters in

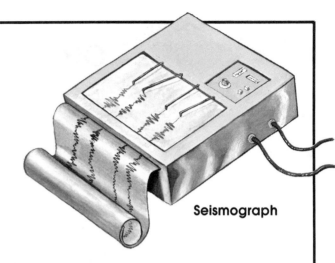

Seismograph

in the sea and on the sea floor.

Computers can organize data far more quickly than people can. Therefore, the information from all the monitoring instruments is transmitted to a huge computer center at the Observatory.

Before it does, the frequency of tremors and earthquakes will probably increase. The water level in nearby wells and springs should drop. The temperature of gas and steam spouting from the crater ought to rise dramatically. The mountain itself may change shape slightly as the magma rises inside.

With their highly sensitive instruments, scientists should be able to detect these signs in time to warn the people who live on Mt. Vesuvius. In the meantime, the only safe prediction is that the mountain will erupt in the near future. Paolo Gasparini, former director of the Mt. Vesuvius Observatory, recently issued this grave warning:

*There will be an eruption, maybe sooner, maybe later, but it will happen... and it will happen soon.*

These words are a grim reminder of the warning first issued by the Viceroy of Naples more than 350 years ago.

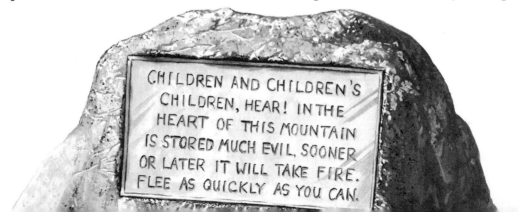

CHILDREN AND CHILDREN'S CHILDREN, HEAR! IN THE HEART OF THIS MOUNTAIN IS STORED MUCH EVIL, SOONER OR LATER IT WILL TAKE FIRE. FLEE AS QUICKLY AS YOU CAN.

# Glossary

The glossary contains definitions and phonetic pronunciations for special, uncommon, or foreign words used in this book.

**aedile**........................[a-**DEAL**] (Latin) The second-highest elected official in a Roman city such as Pompeii.

**amphitheater** ...............[**AM**-fah-thee-uh-ter] A coliseum or Roman stadium.

**archaeology** .................[are-key-**ALL**-o-gee] The recovery and study of material from past civilizations.

**atrium**.......................[**A**-tree-um] The front court of a Roman house. Usually a large open room with an opening in the roof for sunlight.

**barbarian** ...................[bar-**BARE**-ee-un] One who belongs to a people or tribe that is considered uncivilized, primitive, or savage.

**basilica**.....................[ba-**SILL**-ick-ka] A round or oblong building like those built by ancient Romans as courts of justice.

**cone** .........................A mountain of lava, ash, and other volcanic material that builds up around the crater of a volcano.

**colonnade** ...................[call-o-**NADE**] A row of columns, often used to support the roof of a building.

**crust** .......................The top layer of the earth's surface, composed of rock about 50 miles thick (80 kilometers) and divided into several plates.

**decurion**.....................[day-**CURE**-ee-un] (Latin) A city council member in a Roman city such as Pompeii.

**duovirion**....................[duo-**VEER**-ee-un] (Latin) The highest elected official in a Roman city such as Pompeii.

**eruption** . . . . . . . . . . . . . . . . . . . . The release of magma from a volcano, or the release of steam or mud from a geyser.

**equestrian** . . . . . . . . . . . . . . . . . [e-**QUEST**-tree-un] A high-ranking military officer of the Roman Empire. Also a member of the Roman Order of Equestrians.

**excavate** . . . . . . . . . . . . . . . . . . . [**EX**-cah-vate] To uncover by digging.

**flow** . . . . . . . . . . . . . . . . . . . . . . . The second phase of a glowing avalanche caused by an explosive volcanic eruption. The flow is a deadly, glowing river of rock melted by temperatures over 700° Fahrenheit (370° Centigrade).

**forum** . . . . . . . . . . . . . . . . . . . . . . The public square at the heart of a Roman city. Citizens usually gathered at the forum to hold public meetings or hear political speeches.

**freedman** . . . . . . . . . . . . . . . . . . . A former slave who has been freed from bondage.

**fresco** . . . . . . . . . . . . . . . . . . . . . . A wall painting done with water colors on fresh plaster.

***garum*** . . . . . . . . . . . . . . . . . . . . . . [**GAR**-um] (Latin) A spicy sauce made from the entrails of fish.

**gladiator** . . . . . . . . . . . . . . . . . . . [**GLAD**-ee-ate-or] A person trained to entertain the public by fighting with another gladiator, often to the death.

**glowing avalanche** . . . . . . . . . . . . A boiling hot mass of pumice, rocks, ash, and debris that rolls down a mountainside after an explosive volcanic eruption.

**Herculaneum** . . . . . . . . . . . . . . . . [her-cue-**LAY**-nee-um] Ancient Roman resort city of about 5000 people located approximately 10 miles (16 kilometers) north of Pompeii. Like Pompeii, it was destroyed and buried by the eruption of Mt. Vesuvius in A.D. 79.

***lanistae*** . . . . . . . . . . . . . . . . . . . . [lah-**NISS**-tay] (Latin) Owners and trainers of gladiators.

*lares* .....................[**LAR**-ays] (Latin) Minor Roman gods believed to protect households from evil.

lava .....................Molten rock that flows from a volcano or crack in the earth's surface.

magma ...................Molten rock under the earth's crust.

magma chamber ..........Underground pockets where magma, or molten rock, is trapped.

*peristyle* .................[**PARE**-uh-style] (Latin) An outdoor courtyard enclosed by the walls of a house.

plate .....................Part of the earth's crust. The crust is divided into several huge plates.

Plinian Eruption ..........[**PLINN**-ee-un e-**RUP**-shun] An explosive volcanic eruption that throws magma, rocks, and ashes high into the air.

pumice ...................[**PUM**-iss] A porous, lightweight rock formed from magma during an explosive volcanic eruption.

*Retiarri* ..................[ret-**TEE**-are-ee] A special type of gladiator armed only with a fisherman's net and a trident.

rhetoric ..................[**RET**-o-rick] The art of public speaking and persuasive use of language.

*Samnite* ..................[**SAM**-night] A special type of gladiator armed with a large sword and shield.

seismograph ..............[**SIZE**-mo-graf] An instrument that measures earthquakes and other ground vibrations.

Senate ...................The governing council of ancient Rome.

senator ..................A member of the Senate.

steward...................A head slave in charge of a Roman household.

*stola* ......................[**STOW**-lah] (Latin) A full-length flowing dress worn by wealthy Roman women.

**surge** ......................The first phase of a glowing avalanche caused by an explosive volcanic eruption. The surge is a boiling cloud of ash, fine rock particles, and poisonous gases.

*thermae* ......................[**THUR**-may] (Latin) Ancient Roman baths.

*Thracian* ......................[**THRAY**-see-un] A special type of gladiator armed with a short sword and small shield.

**tiltmeter** ......................[**TILT**-me-ter] An electronic instrument used to detect and measure subtle changes in land formations.

**toga**......................A draped, one-piece outer garment worn by Roman citizens.

**trident** ......................[**TRY**-dent) A long spear with three sharp, pointed prongs.

**tunic** ......................A simple, loose-fitting knee-length shirt.

**vent** ......................A gap or weak area in the earth's crust through which magma, or molten rock, rises to the earth's surface.

**vestibule** ......................[**VEST**-ib-yule] Entryway or small lobby.

**viceroy** ......................[**VICE**-roy] Governor of a state, province, territory, or colony.

**villa** ......................A Roman country estate, which included a farm and a home.

**volcanologist** ......................[vol-cun-**ALL**-o-jist] A scientist who studies volcanoes.

# Suggestions for Further Reading

## POMPEII

Andrews, Ian. *Pompeii*. New York: Cambridge University Press, 1978.

"Buried for Centuries." *National Geographic World*, August 1985, pp. 1219.

Gore, Rick. "After 2,000 Years of Silence, the Dead Do Tell Tales at Vesuvius." *National Geographic*, May 1984, pp. 556-613.

Goor, Ron and Nancy. *Pompeii: Exploring a Roman Ghost Town*. New York: Thomas Y. Crowell, 1986.

Hills, C. A. *The Destruction of Pompeii and Herculaneum*. New York: Batsford Company, 1987.

Judge, Joseph. "A Buried Roman Town Gives Up Its Dead." *National Geographic*, December 1982, pp. 687-693.

Maiuri, Amedeo. "Last Moments of the Pompeiians." *National Geographic*, November 1961, pp. 651-669.

## ROMAN CIVILIZATION

Christ, Carl. *The Romans*. Berkeley: University of California Press, 1984.

Forman, Joan, and Harry Strongman. *The Romans*. Englewood Cliffs, New Jersey: Silver Burdett, 1977.

Hodge, Peter. *Roman Towns*. White Plains, New York: Longman, 1977.

## VOLCANOES

Ericson, Jon. *Volcanoes and Earthquakes*. Blue Ridge Summit, Pennsylvania: TAB Books, 1988.

Fodor, R. V. *Earth Afire!* New York: William Morrow and Company, 1981.

Francis, Peter. *Volcanoes*. New York: Penguin Books, 1976.

Lambert, M. B. *Volcanoes*. Seattle: University of Washington Press, 1978.

Rittman, A. and J. *Volcanoes*. New York: Putnam's, 1976.

Time-Life, eds. *Volcano*. Alexandria, Virginia: Time-Life Books, 1982.

# Other Works Consulted

Balsden, J. P. *Roman Women*. London: Bodley Head, 1962.

Barrow, Reginald H. *The Romans*. Chicago: Aldine Publishing Company, 1975.

Brion, Marcel. *Pompeii and Herculaneum: The Glory and the Grief*. John Rosenberg, tr. London: P. Elek, 1960.

Carcopino, Jerome. *Daily Life in Ancient Rome*. E.O. Lorimer, tr. New Haven, Connecticut: Yale University Press, 1955.

Church, Alfred J. *Roman Life in the Days of Cicero*. New York: Biblo and Tannen, 1966.

D'Arms, John H. *Romans on the Bay of Naples*. Cambridge, Massachusetts: Harvard University Press, 1970.

Durant, William. *Caesar and Christ: A History of Roman Civilization*. New York: Simon and Schuster, 1944.

Goodenough, Simon. *Citizens of Rome*. New York: Crown Publishers, 1979.

Grant, Michael. *The Art and Life of Pompeii and Herculaneum*. New York: Newsweek, Inc., 1979.

Pliny the Younger. *Letters, and Panegyricus*. Betty Radice, tr. Cambridge, Massachusetts: Harvard University Press, 1969.

Rawson, Beryl, ed. *The Family in Ancient Rome*. Ithaca, New York: Cornell University Press, 1987.

Rowell, Henry T. *Rome in the Augustan Age*. Norman, Oklahoma: University of Oklahoma Press, 1985.

# INDEX

**The Author**, Timothy Levi Biel was born and raised in eastern Montana. A graduate of Rocky Mountain College, he received a Ph.D. in literary studies from Washington State University.

He is the author of numerous nonfiction books, many of which are part of the highly acclaimed Zoobooks series for young readers. In addition, he has written *The Black Death: World Disasters* and is the editor of the World Disaster Series.

**The Designer**, Walter Stuart was born in San Diego, where he now makes his home. After graduating from San Diego State University and attending the Cleveland Institute of Art, he received an M.A. in biomedical communication from the University of Texas. His illustrations and designs have been featured in nearly fifty books.

**The Illustrator**, Chris Miller was born in San Diego, where he has lived and worked most of his life. Self-taught, he has studied and trained himself in the classical tradition.

His work has won numerous awards, including a first prize from the World Fantasy Convention in 1981. Currently, he is the chief illustrator for the World Disaster Series.